This book belongs to

Natasha O.

From mamy
merry x-mas / 1990

A
BOOK
IS A PRESENT

YOU CAN OPEN
AGAIN
AND
AGAIN

This Book Belongs To

Natasha

© Mary Engelbreit

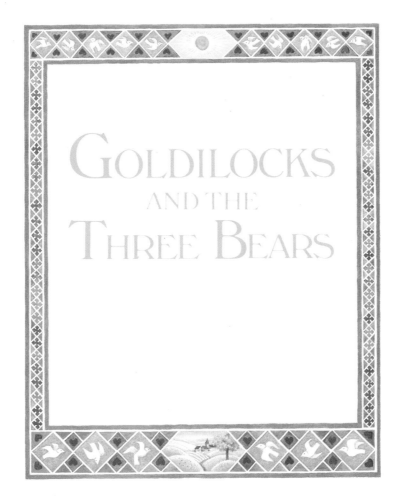

GOLDILOCKS
AND THE
THREE BEARS

THIS IS A BORZOI BOOK
PUBLISHED BY ALFRED A. KNOPF, INC.

Library of Congress Cataloging-in-Publication Data

Eisen, Armand.
Goldilocks and the three bears.

Adaptation of: Three bears.
Summary: Lost in the woods, a tired and hungry little girl finds the house of
the three bears where she helps herself to food and goes to sleep.
[1. Folklore. 2. Bears—Folklore] I. Ferris, Lynn, ill. II. Three bears.
III. Title.
PZ8.1.E35GO   1987   398.2'1   [E]   86-46154
ISBN 0-394-55882-0

Manufactured in Singapore
Published October 30, 1987
Second Printing, June 1989

A NOTE ON THE TYPE

The text of this book was set in a digitized version of Garamond No. 3, a
modern rendering of the type first cut by Claude Garamond (c. 1480–1561).
It is believed that Garamond based his letters on the Venetian models,
although he introduced a number of important differences, and it is to him
we owe the letter which we know as "old style."

Composed by Maxwell Photographics, Inc., New York, New York

Separations, printing, and binding by Tien Wah Press, Singapore

Art direction by Armand Eisen and Thomas Durwood

Designed by Marysarah Quinn

The artwork in this book is dedicated
to my mother and father.

L.B.F.

They had only been gone a short while when along came a little girl named Goldilocks. She was gathering wild flowers in the field next to the big woods. "There must be some more flowers beyond those trees," thought Goldilocks. So she walked into the forest and had not gone far when she saw the three bears' cottage. "Oh, how pretty!" Goldilocks said to herself, "I wonder who lives there?"

Goldilocks peered in the window. Nobody was home, so she opened the door and went right in.

The first thing she saw was a table with three bowls of porridge on it: a great big bowl for Papa Bear, a medium-sized bowl for Mama Bear, and a tiny little bowl for Baby Bear. Goldilocks was feeling hungry, so she tasted the porridge in the great big bowl.

"Ouch!" she cried, dropping the spoon. "This porridge is too hot!"

Then she tasted the porridge in the medium-sized bowl. "Oh!" she cried, making a face. "This porridge is too cold!"

Then she tasted the porridge in the tiny little bowl. "Mmmm...This porridge is just right!" And she ate it all up!

By then, Goldilocks was feeling tired. Seeing three chairs, she thought, "I'll just sit down for a little bit."

She climbed into the great big chair that belonged to Papa Bear. "Oh!" she cried, jumping down. "This chair is much too hard!"

Then she tried Mama Bear's chair. "Humph," she said. "This one is much too soft."

Then she went over to the tiny little chair that belonged to Baby Bear. "This one looks just right."

But do you know what happened as soon as she sat down in it? Crack! The little chair broke!

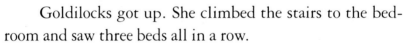

Goldilocks got up. She climbed the stairs to the bed-room and saw three beds all in a row.

"I am sleepy!" she said, yawning.

And so she pulled down the covers and climbed right into Papa Bear's great big bed! But it was too hard.

Then she climbed into Mama Bear's medium-sized bed. But that was too soft!

Then she climbed into Baby Bear's tiny little bed, which was just right. And what do you think happened then? Why, Goldilocks fell fast asleep!